Walt Disney's

The Ugly Duckling

Retold by Margaret Wise Brown

Illustrated by Gil DiCicco

DISNEY PRESS

NEW YORK

This text originally appeared in the collection entitled *Little Pig's Picnic and Other Stories*, published by D. C. Heath and Company.

ISBN 0-7868-3007-7/0-7868-5001-9

Once upon a time there were two ducks. They had their nest on the edge of a pond in a far corner of the world. In the nest were five round, smooth eggs.

When the mother duck wasn't sitting on the nest, the father duck was sitting on the nest. All the time they were waiting for some little ducklings to come out of the eggs.

They waited for a long time. The father duck walked up and down. He walked up and down so much that he wore a deep path in the earth where he walked.

And then one day there came a pick-pick-pick from inside the eggs. And, one by one, out tumbled four tiny yellow ducklings. When they came tumbling over the edge of the nest, the father duck looked at them with pride and joy.

Then there came a pick-pick-pick from inside the fifth egg. Out tumbled the fifth duckling!

There he stood on one foot. He did not look like the others. His feathers were white instead of yellow. His neck was longer. His eyes were big and staring.

When the other ducklings saw him, they ran and hid under their mother's wing. The mother duck stood there and looked. Never had she hatched a duck like this before.

The father duck came running over with a quack-quack-quack.

"Where did this little thing come from?" he asked. "*You* must have laid that egg," said the mother duck. "I don't lay eggs!" said the father duck. "Quack! Quack! Quack! Where did this little thing come from?"

The little thing stood there with a piece of eggshell on his head like a hat. He looked around him for the first time. He was so very happy to be born. He looked at the tall green grasses and the pink water lilies of the brand-new world he was living in. He did not know he was an ugly duckling.

Then the mother duck took her little ducklings for their first walk. She shooed the yellow ducklings on before her. The ugly duckling came waddling along behind. But when he tried to come close to the mother duck, she shooed him away.

"You're no child of mine," she seemed to say. Still, the ugly duckling tagged along.

When the ducklings went for their first swim, the ugly duckling paddled his legs under him right along with the others.

"Well!" said the mother duck. "At least he's a swimming bird. But he certainly is a funny duck. Come, little ducklings, climb onto my back."

The little ducklings climbed onto her back with a quack-quack-quack.

The ugly duckling swam very fast and climbed on, too.
Then he made his first noise.
"Honk! Honk!" he said.
What a strange noise for a duckling!

The mother duck and the little ducklings ducked their heads. Who ever heard of a honking duck! They pushed the ugly duckling off the mother duck's back and into the water. A duck who honked did not belong to them.

Then the mother duck and her ducklings swam off and left the little ugly duckling diving around by himself. He was very lonesome.

He only looked back once at the yellow-feathered backs of the other ducklings as they ran after their mother. Then he went away all by himself.

The poor little duckling swam and swam until he was
very tired. Then he climbed up onto the dry land.

Standing there, he looked down into the dark blue
water. There in the water was his reflection, all twisted by
the ripples of the stream. He did not look like the other
ducklings. His eyes were too big, and his neck was too
long. His feathers were white instead of yellow.

And then he knew. He was an ugly duckling. Big tears
came out of his eyes and fell on the ground.

Poor little duckling! Another big tear squeezed out of
one eye.

He was not wanted. He was an ugly duckling, and nobody loved him. So he wandered off all alone through the marshes—one little duck in the wide, wide world.

As he walked along, he did not see that the rushes grew green by the bank, and red-winged blackbirds were singing in the sunlight.

Suddenly he heard a chirping. Looking up, he saw four friendly little marsh birds chirping to him from a nest in a fallen tree.

The ugly duckling gave a little honk and climbed right up into the nest with them. The baby birds chirped lovingly around him. The nest was warm, and the little birds were soft beside him.

All at once the little birds opened their bills, and along came flying the old marsh bird who was their mother. She had a big worm, which she threw to them for their supper.

But when the ugly duckling caught it, the mother bird squawked with rage and pulled the worm away.

She chased the duckling from her nest, pecked him on the head, and beat him with her wings.

The little duckling ran and ran until he jumped into the water. Then he swam away as fast as he could. He swam so fast that he bumped right smack into a wooden duck and started it rocking.

When the ugly duckling saw the big wooden duck, he rubbed his little head against the duck's wooden breast.

He didn't know that it was just a wooden duck painted in wild-bird colors. He didn't know that the wooden duck was put there by hunters to lure *real* wild ducks!

He simply thought, Here is a friend.

The wooden duck did not swim away from him. Instead it let the ugly duckling climb up onto the end of its tail and bounce up and down there.

He was so happy that he gave a big bounce in the air that landed him in the water. This tipped the wooden duck so far forward that when it rocked back again, it smacked the little duckling on the head.

The ugly duckling thought his new friend had knocked into him on purpose, so he swam off down the stream, the saddest little duck in all the world.

He hid in the reeds that grew along the riverbank and honked as though his little heart would break. His tears fell into the water and made little circles there. He stopped to watch one tear hit the water. Then he put his head down on the ground and cried and cried.

Just then a great white mother swan and her four little swans came floating down the river.

They stopped and listened when they heard the little duck honking on the shore. And when the little swans saw the ugly duckling with his head down on the ground, they came swimming over to him.

"Honk! Honk! Honk!" the swans called to him.

When he heard the sound, the ugly duckling looked around and saw the four baby swans. They were as white as he was, and they all had long necks like his own. They were honking to him in a friendly way. He was so happy he dove right into his own reflection in the water and broke it.

When he came up, the little swans were still there.
The young swans played with him and swam in circles around him.

Then the great white mother swan honked to the little swans. The ugly duckling looked up and saw her. Never had he seen such a beautiful white curving bird.

The baby swans all went swimming back to the great white swan. The little duckling watched them go. He wished he might grow up to be beautiful like these swans. Then he remembered he was an ugly duckling. His little head dropped, and he started to swim off by himself, all alone on the wide waters of the stream.

But the swans would not let him go. They knew that the ugly duckling was really a baby swan, just like them. So the white swans swam around the little lost swan and stroked his neck with their beaks. The mother let him come near to the soft swan's down on her breast.